# MADAGASCAR

## ESCAPE 2 AFRICA™

# AIR PENGUIN

Adapted by Gail Herman
Pencils by Charles Grosvenor
Paintings by Lydia Halverson

HarperCollins *Children's Books*

The animals from the New York zoo
are leaving Madagascar.

"You've been a great crowd!"

Alex calls to the lemurs.

"Goodbye! Goodbye!"

say Marty, Melman, and Gloria.

Skipper and the penguins stand
at the controls of an old aeroplane.
"Doors?" asks Skipper.
"Check!" says Kowalski.
Holiday in Madagascar? Over.

Mason and Phil, the chimps,

don't look up.

They're too busy playing chess.

"This is your captain speaking,"
Skipper tells everyone.
"We'd like you to sit back, relax,
and hope this hunk of junk flies!"
Rico gives the signal.

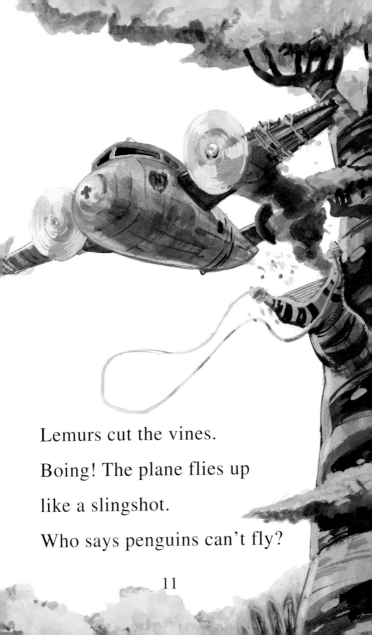

Lemurs cut the vines.

Boing! The plane flies up

like a slingshot.

Who says penguins can't fly?

Over Africa, Kowalski spots trouble.

A red light flashes. Danger!

"Rico!" Skipper orders.

"Instruction manual!"

Rico hands over the book.

Skipper smashes the light with it.

"Problem solved!" he says.

Boom! One engine goes out.

Boom! The second engine goes out.

Something is wrong,

and it isn't the light!

"Buckle up, boys!" says Skipper.

"We're coming in for a landing!"

The plane crashes through trees.

The wings and the tail rip off.

The aeroplane drops.

"Ahhhhh!" scream the animals.

Quickly the penguins open parachutes.

Whoosh!

The plane floats to the ground.

"Hey, happy slappers!" says Alex.

"The plane is a wreck.

How are you going to fix it?"

"With grit, spit,

and a lot of tape!" Skipper says.

17

People on a safari tour ride past.

"They'll help us," roars Alex.

But no one understands his roaring.

"You're a bad kitty!"

says a mean old lady named Nana.

"Who needs people?" Skipper says.

"We're penguins!

We need aeroplane parts.

And a plan!"

The penguins have an idea.

"We'll take a truck!" says Skipper.

Private pretends he's been hit.

Screech! The truck stops.

"He's hurt!" says the driver.

The people rush out of the truck.

The penguins jump into the truck.

"Good work, boys!" says Skipper
as they drive away.

The penguins take more trucks.

They strip off metal.

They pull out plugs and wires.

Now they have
plenty of parts
to fix the aeroplane.

But it's not easy fixing a plane
when you have flippers.
"Where are our thumbs?"
says Skipper.

Just then, Phil and Mason show up.

They have thumbs!

Their friends have thumbs, too.

"Well, I'll be a monkey's uncle,"

says Skipper.

Suddenly, Marty gallops over.

"The plane!" he pants.

"Need it! For a rescue mission!

Alex is in trouble!"

But the plane isn't ready.

The penguins need more spit here

and more grit there.

And lots and lots of tape!

Can it be fixed in time?

At last! The plane is ready.

Everyone gets into place.

The penguins put on snappy music.

The chimps eat bananas

to help them power the propellers.

The engine roars.

The plane flies over the trees.

The chimps help Alex escape!

"It's you!" Nana yells

at the penguins.

"What did you expect?" asks Skipper.

"A barrel of monkeys?"

Now everyone is safe.

The penguins fly the four friends

back to the water hole.

Mission? Complete!

"Thank you for flying Air Penguin,"
Skipper says.

"Now sit back, pipe down,
and enjoy the trip!"